FOR
CASPER
ATLAS
GEURTS

First US edition 2022

Library of Congress Catalog Card Number pending
ISBN 978-1-5362-2045-2

21 22 23 24 25 26 27 APS 10 9 8 7 6 5 4 3 2 1

Printed in Humen, Dongguan, China

This book was typeset in Gill Sans MT Pro Light.
The illustrations were done in cut paper and ink.

Candlewick Press
99 Dover Street
Somerville, Massachusetts 02144

www.candlewick.com

# BEE

Charlotte Voake

CANDLEWICK PRESS

This is a beehive, where the honeybees live.
On warm spring days I watch them flying
in and out, in and out.

"What do you do in that hive all day?
Where do you go when
you leave?" I ask.

Then one day, I heard a tiny voice say,
"I have the striped trousers, Bella,"
and another tiny voice say,
"I have the furry
jacket, Beatrice.
But how will
they fit
him?"

"Magic!" whispered Beatrice.

The two honeybees had brought a little suit for ME!

The next minute I was the size
of a teeny-weeny honeybee,
wearing my new outfit!

At the entrance to the hive
a guard called out,
"Hey, he's not one of us!"

"Please let him in," said Bella.
"We're giving him a guided tour."

It was pitch-black
inside the beehive, but luckily
I had a tiny flashlight.

"Would you mind putting that light out?"
asked Bella. "We like to work
in the dark."

It was very hot in there, and I could
hardly see a thing, but it smelled
LOVELY.

"Honey," said
Beatrice.

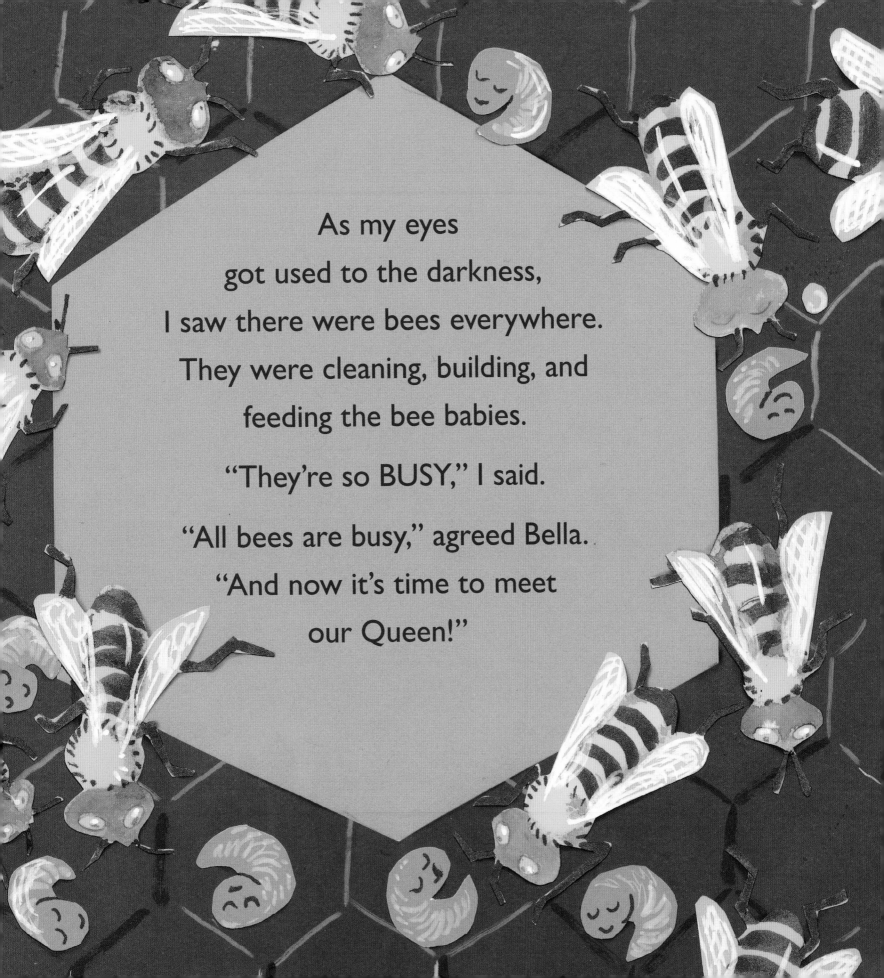

As my eyes
got used to the darkness,
I saw there were bees everywhere.
They were cleaning, building, and
feeding the bee babies.

"They're so BUSY," I said.

"All bees are busy," agreed Bella.
"And now it's time to meet
our Queen!"

When we found the Queen,
little bees were brushing her
glossy coat and polishing
her beautiful wings.

"She is the mother of us all,"
Beatrice said.
I bowed to the Queen.
The Queen looked down at me.
"Hmmm," she said. "He's not one of us,
but I like his suit!"

Suddenly we heard a loud buzzing in the hive.

I was a bit frightened.

"That's Brenda dancing!" shouted Bella above the noise.

"The waggle dance shows us where to find flowers."

Everyone headed

for the door.

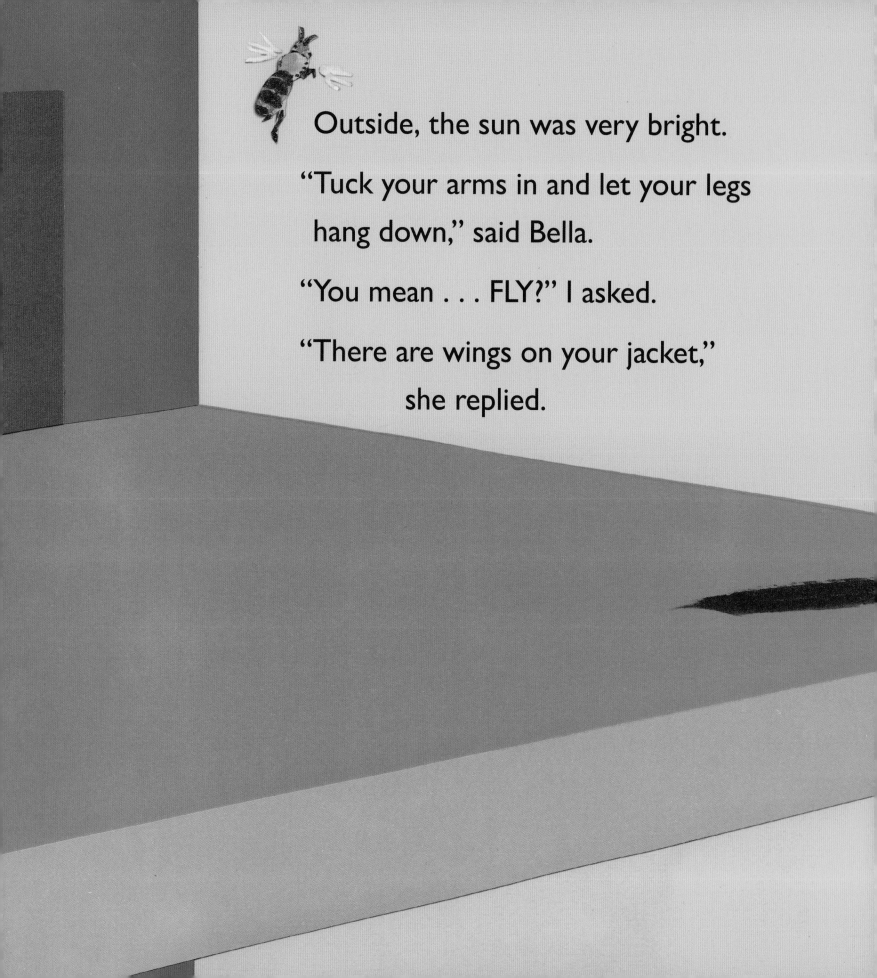

Outside, the sun was very bright.

"Tuck your arms in and let your legs hang down," said Bella.

"You mean . . . FLY?" I asked.

"There are wings on your jacket," she replied.

I practiced my flying. Our wings were going so fast, we could hardly see them!

"You'll soon get the hang of it," said Beatrice.

Down on the street no one noticed us,
except for a little girl.

"I just saw a tiny boy in a bee suit," she said.

"We must hurry," replied her mother,
"or we'll miss our bus."

At last we reached a big patch of plants.

"Strawberries!" Beatrice exclaimed.
I could hardly see any strawberries.

"The flowers are
what we like!"
she said.

Beatrice showed me how to find
the sugary juice inside the flowers.
Mmm—it was sweet!

"That's nectar," said the bees. "We take
it home and make it
into honey."

Sometimes it is hard to find
flowers in the city.
But we found one
in a crack in the pavement.

"Every flower counts,"
said Bella.

We were covered in yellow dust.

"Pollen," explained Beatrice.

"The babies LOVE it!"

It was late when
I said goodbye
to my new friends.

"Thank you for lending
me the suit . . .

I'm afraid the wings
are a bit worn out."

The minute I took

off the little suit . . .

I was **BIG** again!

"Good night, Bella. Good night, Beatrice," I said quietly.

"Tomorrow I'm going to do something

for YOU."

So I planted lots of seeds and flowers,

and the bees loved them.

Because every flower counts . . .

for
every little
bee!